The Honeybee

This book has been reviewed
for accuracy by
Walter L. Gojmerac
Professor of Entomology
University of Wisconsin—Madison.

Library of Congress Cataloging in Publication Data

Otani, Takeshi.
 The honeybee.

 (Nature close-ups)
 Translation of: Mitsubachi / text by Takeshi Otani,
photographs by Satoshi Kuribayashi.
 Summary: Discusses the life cycle, behavior patterns,
and habitats of honeybees.
 1. Honeybee—Juvenile literature. [1. Honeybee.
2. Bees] I. Kuribayashi, Satoshi, 1939-   , ill.
II. Title. III. Series.
 QL568.A608413 1986   595.79'9   85-28230

ISBN 0-8172-2537-4 (lib. bdg.)
ISBN 0-8172-2562-5 (softcover)

This edition first published in 1986 by Raintree Publishers

Text copyright © 1986 by Raintree Publishers Limited Partnership,
translated from *Honeybee* copyright © 1981 by Takeshi Ohtani.

Photographs copyright © 1981 by Satoshi Kuribayashi.

World English translation rights for *Color Photo Books on Nature*
arranged with Kaisei-Sha through Japan Foreign-Rights Center.

4 5 6 7 8 9 10   99 98 97 96 95 94 93 92 91 90

The Honeybee

Raintree Publishers
Milwaukee

◀ **Bees swarming in a summer sky.**

Honeybees are called social insects because they live and work together in large groups. A large swarm of bees searches for a new home when the old hive becomes too crowded.

▶ **A swarm of bees resting on a tree branch.**

Up to half the worker bees in the old hive will fly off with a queen bee in search of a new home. The other bees stay behind to care for remaining bee larvae and the new queen, which is already developing.

Honeybees live together in large groups called colonies. When a colony of honeybees becomes too crowded, worker bees and a queen leave the old nest, or hive, to find a new home. The bees' flight to form a new colony is called swarming. Swarming often takes place in early summer.

The swarming bees often mass together on a fence post or tree branch, and scouts go out to look for a new home. Sometimes bees scout for a new home even before they leave the old hive. Bees build their nests in places that are sheltered from the wind and rain. They choose places like hollow trees or caves or wooden hives provided by beekeepers.

Of the ten thousand kinds, or species, of bees, only one species makes honey. Honeybees are the only insects in the world to produce food which is eaten by people.

◀ Worker bees begin to build a honeycomb.

▶ Wax secreted from glands in the bee's abdomen (left photo, top) and pieces of wax (right photo, top).

The bee uses its back legs to remove the pieces of wax from its abdomen. Then it chews the wax, which becomes a cloudy white color, and uses it to shape the cells in the comb.

Once the new location has been found, the worker bees immediately begin to build a comb in their new home. In the back section of the body, the abdomen, honeybees have special glands that secrete wax. Using the wax and working together, the bees rapidly construct a series of small, six-sided cells, called a honeycomb. The workers build the comb from the top of the hive downward. First the floor is laid, then the walls begin to appear. In two days' time, a number of combs, with cells on both sides, have been completed. Eventually, there will be many thousands of cells in the hive.

◀ Cells being constructed on both sides at the base of the comb.

▶ A worker removes another bee's wax.

Because these bees are linked together as they build the comb, they cannot remove the wax from their own abdomens. Another worker bites off the wax and uses it.

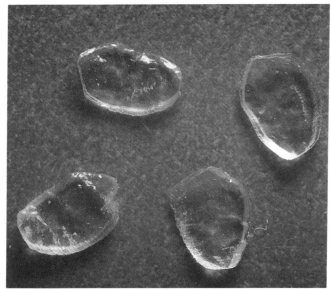

◄ **A honeycomb under construction.**

The queen may deposit an egg in a cell before the sides are completely built. Workers continue to add wax and build up the walls while the egg is in the cell, waiting to hatch.

▶ **Sealed honey cells (top), yellow pollen cells (middle), and cells for developing bees (bottom).**

The lower brood cells, capped with brown wax, are where the bee pupae are developing. Above them are the storage cells that contain white and yellow pollen. In the sealed cells above, honey is stored.

In the cells built by the workers, food is stored, helpless young bees are cared for, and the queen is attended. In the center of the hive, the warmest part of the nest, are the brood cells. This is where the queen lays her eggs and the young bees develop. Pollen is stored in cells next to and above the brood cells. And outside and above the pollen cells, nectar is stored. The stored nectar later turns into honey.

◄ **A wooden hive and combs.**

The black arrow shows the combs in this beekeeper's hive. The lid and a side board have been removed. The white arrow indicates the entrance/exit to the hive.

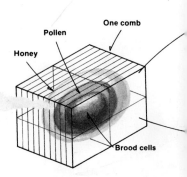

One comb
Pollen
Honey
Brood cells

When you remove the combs, you will find:

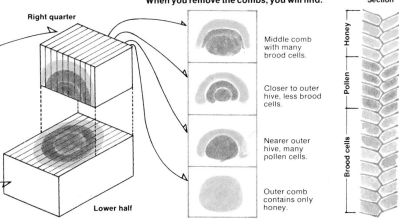

Right quarter

Lower half

Middle comb with many brood cells.

Closer to outer hive, less brood cells.

Nearer outer hive, many pollen cells.

Outer comb contains only honey.

Section

Honey

Pollen

Brood cells

● **The hive's interior.**

The cells inside the hive are arranged so that the brood cells in the center are surrounded by the pollen and honey cells. This helps to protect the young developing bees from changes in weather and other dangers.

◀ **A queen with her royal circle.**

As the queen lays her eggs, she is constantly surrounded by the royal circle, six to ten young workers who regularly feed and groom her. As she moves about, searching for clean, empty cells in which to lay her eggs, some workers leave the royal circle, others join it.

▶ **The queen bee lays an egg.**

Surrounded by workers, the queen bee inserts her abdomen into an empty cell. A few seconds later, pushing down deep into the cell, she lays her egg, then carefully withdraws her abdomen.

The queen is a very special member of the bee colony. Worker bees have a number of duties, but the queen has only one job—to lay eggs. She is the only bee in the hive who performs that task. On a busy day she may lay up to 1,500 eggs. The queen lives longer than any bee in the hive—up to five or six years. In her lifetime, she may lay a million eggs.

In addition to the queen and worker bees, male drones also live in the hive. These large bees do not work, cannot sting, and will not even feed themselves. The drone's only purpose in life is to mate with a young queen bee.

● **Body parts of worker, drone, and queen bee.**

Size, shape, and length of honeybees vary. The worker is less than one-half inch long, while the queen measures almost an inch.

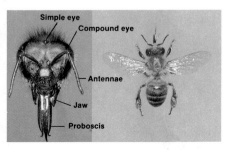

Worker

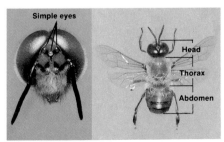

Drone

Queen

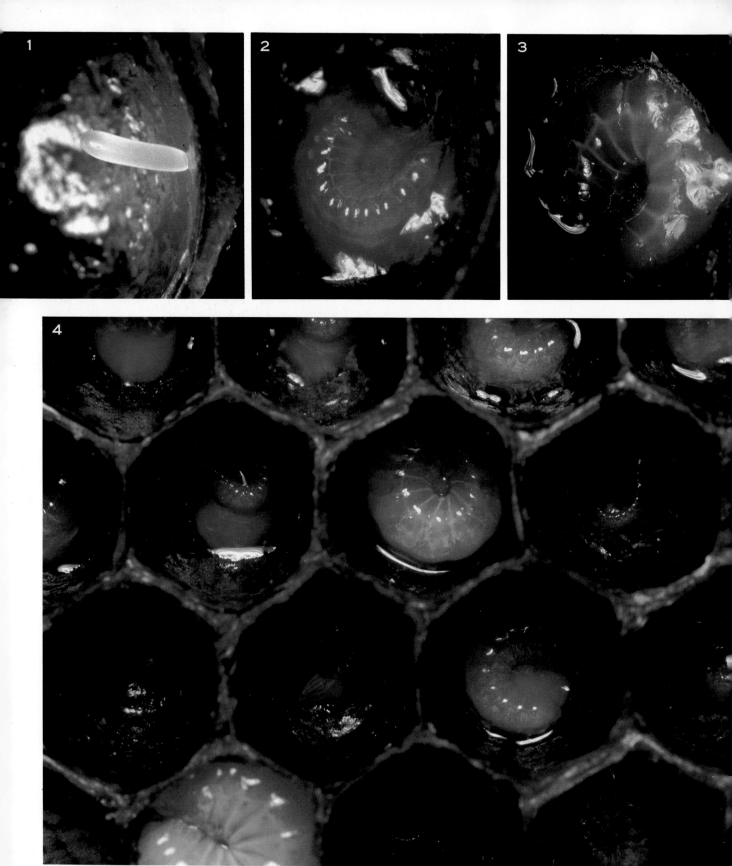

◄ **Development of an egg into a larva (photos 1-4).**

The honeybee egg is white, banana-shaped, and about as big as the dot over an *i*. When the egg hatches, the tiny larva bends into a U-shape and floats on a bed of royal jelly from which it feeds. Below is a diagram that explains photo 4.

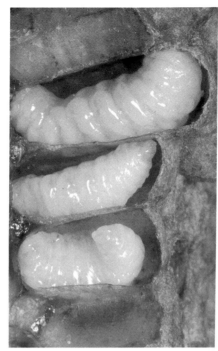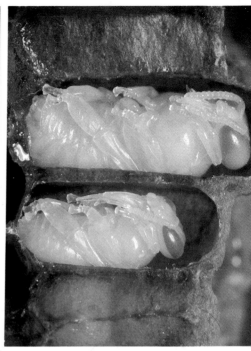

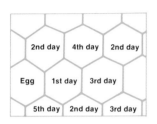

2nd day	4th day	2nd day
Egg	1st day	3rd day
5th day	2nd day	3rd day

● **Larvae about to become pupae (left) and in the pupal stage (right).**

When it has spun a silk covering, the larva lies motionless in a curved position and enters the pupal, or resting, stage. The large pupa at the top has developed from an unfertilized egg and it will become a drone.

Like many insects, bees go through four stages of development: egg, larva, pupa, and adult. It takes twenty-one days for a worker bee to develop from an egg into an adult. On the third day after the queen lays the egg, a tiny, worm-like larva crawls out. It is fed a creamy jelly by the worker bees. The jelly, called royal jelly, is rich in vitamins and protein. It is produced by glands in the heads of week-old adult workers. When the larva is three days old, the workers begin feeding it "beebread," a mixture of pollen and honey.

By the time it is six days old, the larva is fully grown, so the worker bees seal the cell with wax. The larva spins a silk covering for itself and rests in this pupal stage for the next twelve days. During this time, many changes take place, as the pupa becomes an adult.

▼ A worker bee emerges from its cell. When it is fully developed and has shed its pupal skin, the adult bee emerges. Although its wings are fully developed, the bee cannot fly until they have hardened.

▶ **Older workers greet the young bees.**

The older workers greet the young bees by touching them with their antennae. The body hairs of the young bees are whitish and ruffled and their abdomens are light in color, making them easy to distinguish from the older bees.

As the time nears for the developing bees to leave, or emerge from, their cells, the workers shave away some of the wax from the outside of the seals. By doing so, the workers make it easier for the bees inside to come out. One after the other, the young adult bees chew through the caps of their cells and emerge to the outer world of the hive.

Female workers greet the young bees by touching them with their feelers, or antennae. The young bees, whose wings have not yet hardened, cannot fly about, searching for food. So, the older workers, who have collected nectar from flowers, share it with the young bees. The nectar, stored in the workers' social stomach, or crop, is regurgitated and fed to the young bees.

The young worker bee cleans her needle-like mouth, called a proboscis, by rubbing it with her front legs. After the young bees have cleaned themselves, they begin to clean and polish the empty brood cells so the queen can lay eggs in them.

The young worker bees begin their busy lives immediately. At first, they work in the middle part of the hive, taking care of various activities in the brood nest. After carefully cleaning themselves, the new workers crawl into the empty cells to polish the walls and floors so that the queen can lay eggs in them once again. And, just as these newly emerged bees were once cared for by other workers, it is now their turn to look after the developing larvae and pupae in the nest. The young workers feed the larvae royal jelly at first, and later, beebread. And when the larvae have developed to the pupal stage, the young workers seal the cells with wax. Later, when the young bees inside are ready to emerge, the workers help them by shaving off some of the wax cap.

▶ Various activities of the young worker bees (photos 1-6).

(1) Two young bees receiving nectar from another worker (bee on right). (2) A bee regurgitating nectar which she will store in a honey cell for later use. (3) A worker feeding a drone (bee on top). (4) Workers feeding the queen (bee in center). (5) Workers feeding the developing larvae. (6) Workers sealing the cells of the mature larvae.

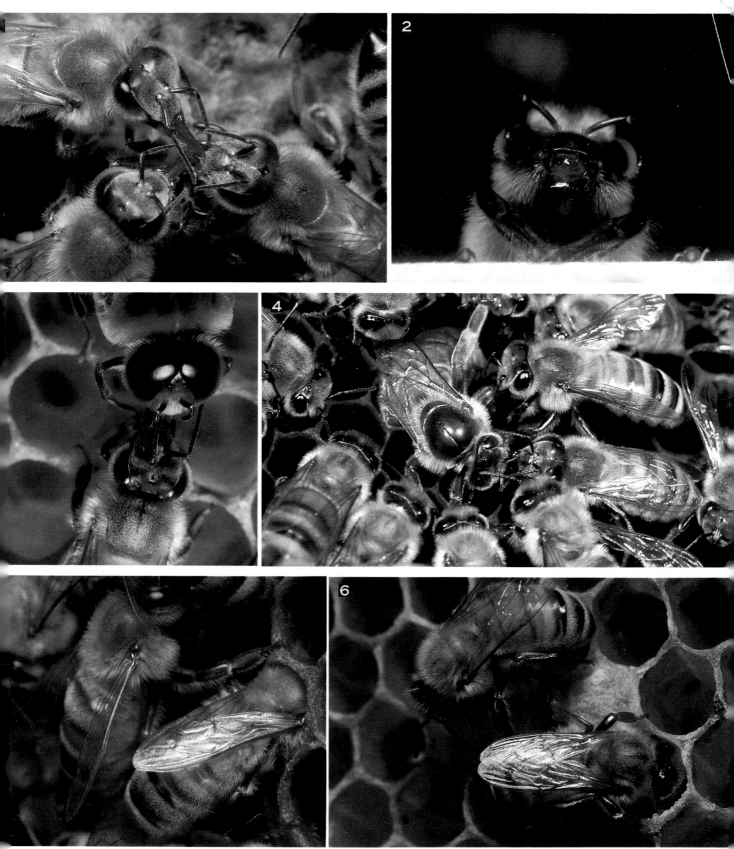

◀ **A worker bee carries out a dead pupa.**

Removing things like dead pupae and dirt from the hive is one of the many tasks worker bees do.

▶ **Worker bees forming a ladder.**

Using the claws on their legs, these worker bees attach themselves to one another to form a chain ladder from one honeycomb to another. Other bees climb up the ladder to build new honeycombs and perform other tasks.

As they get older, the workers move to jobs in the outer area of the hive. Some do housekeeping tasks like removing dead pupae and other unwanted objects from the hive. Others build new cells. As the number of bees in a hive increases, new cells must be built. Some of the cells are for storing honey. Other cells are built so the queen bee can lay more eggs.

When the worker bees are about three weeks old, they make their first flights outside the hive. They circle the hive on their strong wings and memorize its shape and where it is. This "play flight" helps ensure that later, when they fly off in search of food, they will be able to return to the nest without getting lost.

◀ **Workers fan their wings to cool the hive.**

The brood cells, where the eggs, larvae, and pupae develop, must be at an even temperature. In summer, worker bees fan their wings to cool the hive and keep the temperature at about 93°F. In winter, workers fan their wings to move body heat through the hive and keep the brood area between 50°F and 60°F.

Because the temperature of the brood nest must be fairly even, it is the job of certain worker bees to air condition the hive in summer and heat it in winter. In hot summer weather, workers use their wings to fan air through the hive. If the temperature continues to rise, other worker bees use their proboscises to gather drops of water from outside the hive and deposit them inside. The fanning workers continue to move their wings to spread the cooling effects of the water throughout the hive. In cold weather, workers beat their wings to move the body heat of the other bees in the hive. This helps to keep the queen and the developing bees in the brood nest warm.

◀ A worker bee collecting water.

This worker bee uses its proboscis to gather drops of water from the ground.

● Workers fanning a hive odor from their abdomens.

Workers also use their wings to fan out a scent that is secreted by glands in their abdomens (see black arrows). All the bees in one hive have their own scent. The scent helps other bees find the entrance to the hive. It also helps worker bees who guard the entrance to tell which bees belong in the hive and which do not.

The guard bees let members of the hive enter but drive off stray insects or bees from other hives. The guards identify other members of the hive by their hive odor.

▶ **Giant hornets attack the beehive.**

When hornets attack the hive, the guards alert other workers by producing an alarm scent. Many other worker bees then hurry to the hive's entrance to attack the hornets. If one honeybee fights a hornet, it will probably lose because hornets are much larger.

Some worker bees stand guard at the entrance to the beehive. If other insects or bees from other hives try to enter the hive, the guards quickly attack. Only the worker bees fight battles. They use their barbed stingers as weapons. The guards can emit an alarm scent. Then other bees from inside the hive rush to help the guards. Among the natural enemies of the honeybee are bears, skunks, ants, dragonflies, and in some parts of the world, giant hornets.

◀ **A worker bee's stinger.**

The worker bee's stinger has barbs that point backward. Once a bee has stung a victim, the bee will die. If the bee tries to pull its stinger out, the last segment of its own body will tear off, and it will bleed to death.

● **Worker bees collecting nectar and pollen from flowers.**

(1) A flower of the mint family, (2) a Cosmos flower, (3) a flower of the Compositae family, (4) another Cosmos.

Three weeks after the worker bee has emerged, it is ready to fly off to collect pollen and nectar from flowers. Nectar is rich in sugar and gives the bee energy. Pollen has the same food value for bees that meat and eggs have for people. The bee uses it long, needle-like proboscis to suck up nectar, which it then stores in its crop. As it moves about on the flower, tiny pollen grains stick to the bee's hairy body. The bee rolls the pollen into a ball on its hind legs and carries it back to the nest.

◀ A worker bee carrying balls of pollen.

The plant pollen sticks to hairs on the bee's body. When it rubs its legs together, the pollen collects in a ball on the hind legs. The long hairs on the hind legs form a pollen basket, as shown below.

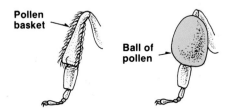

Pollen basket

Ball of pollen

When it returns to the hive, the bee uses its middle legs to scrape off the pollen into the pollen cells that surround the brood cells. It also regurgitates the nectar from its crop and feeds it to other bees. If the bees are fed more nectar than they need, they store the rest in the hive's honey cells. There, as the nectar dries, chemical changes take place, and honey is formed. Later, the workers cap the honey cells with wax.

When a worker finds flowers that will be a good food source, it communicates the location to the other bees in the hive. The worker does so by dancing. If the flowers are close by, the bee dances in a circle. If they are far away, the bee dances in a figure-eight, or "wagtail," dance. The dance tells other bees where the flowers are relative to the position of the sun.

▶ Pollen is stored in the cells.

Piles of pollen are stored for future use. The pollen is different colors because it comes from different flowers. The pollen cells are near the brood cells so that the developing larvae can be easily fed.

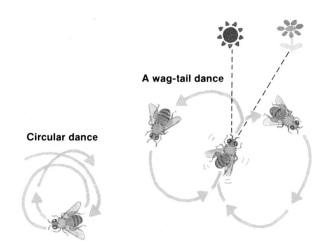

A wag-tail dance

Circular dance

▼ A worker bee performs a dance.

The bee in the middle performs a dance to show where flowers are. The slower the movement of the dancer, the greater the distance to the flowers. With their long feelers, or antennae, the workers smell the scent of the pollen which the dancer carries. Soon they fly off in search of the flowers.

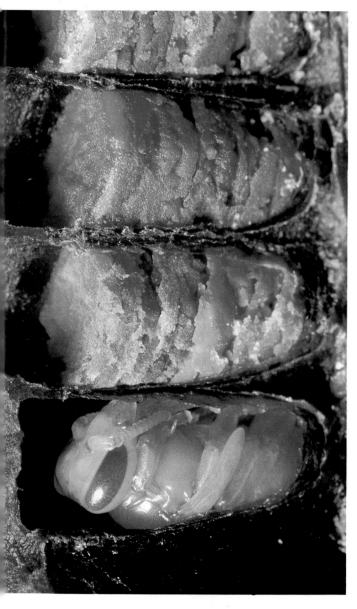

◀ The honey cells are sealed for the winter.

The honeybees use freshly secreted wax when they seal the honey cells. But when the workers seal the cell of a pupa, they usually bite off pieces of wax from the surrounding cells and re-use the wax.

▶ Honeybees crowd together during the winter.

Although their movements have slowed down, the bees often move around in the hive. Those in the outer area of the hive exchange places with those near the center of the hive. But the bees stay close together so no body heat escapes from the hive.

By late autumn, the worker bees have filled the cells in the upper combs with honey and sealed them with wax. The stored honey is precious food for the long winter. In autumn, too, the workers let the drones starve to death. Since the queen does not mate during the winter, the drones are no longer useful. And they would eat some of the winter's food supply needed by the other bees.

To prepare for winter, the workers collect large amounts of a sticky substance called propolis, from trees. They carry this propolis to the hive in their pollen baskets. There they mix it with wax and use this "bee glue" to fill the gaps in the hive to keep out the cold of the coming winter.

Unlike most other insects, honeybees do not hibernate in the winter. However, their body movements slow down. When the cold weather comes, the bees cluster in a mass inside the hive to keep warm.

► Honeybee hives covered with snow.

These wooden beehives are covered by a thick layer of snow. The snow helps to insulate the hives and keeps them warm.

◀ A woodland in early spring.

▶ **Worker bees seek out early spring flowers.**

In the spring, when the snow is melting and the first flowers of the season begin to appear, worker bees begin to search for nectar and pollen. In these photographs, a worker bee is sucking nectar from a coltsfoot (top left); a worker has landed on a camellia (top right); and a worker is hanging from speedwell (bottom).

In early spring, as the snow melts and the first flowers peep out of the ground, the beehive comes to life with a flurry of activity. Only a little of the stored honey remains in the hive. So the first task of the worker bees is to fly off in search of pollen and nectar. The queen immediately begins to lay large quantities of eggs in the empty cells in the hive, and new worker bees soon emerge. In later months, as the colony grows too large, it divides. The old queen and half the workers swarm in search of a new place to establish a home.

A new queen emerges in the old hive. She leaves it briefly and goes on a mating flight. After she mates with a number of drones, she returns to the hive and begins to lay eggs. Year after year, the life cycle of the honeybee continues in this way.

GLOSSARY

abdomen—the back, or rear section, of an insect's body. (pp. 6, 11)

antennae—the movable feelers on an insect's head which detect odor and movement. (pp. 15, 27)

crop—a special storage area for food. Both bees and ants have crops. (pp. 15, 25)

drones—male bees, whose only function is to mate with the queen. (pp. 9, 28, 30)

honeycomb—cells of wax, built by worker honeybees, in which young bees are raised and food is stored. (pp. 6, 18)

larva—the second stage in the life cycle of those insects that go through four definite stages of development: egg, larva, pupa, and adult. (pp. 5, 13, 16)

proboscis—a tube-like mouth which is used for sucking liquids. (pp. 16, 20, 25)

propolis—a resin-like material collected from trees by bees and used as glue to seal the opening of the beehive. (p. 28)

pupa—the third stage in the life cycle of those insects that go through four definite stages of development. During this resting stage, the body of the adult insect is forming. Often, the pupa is enclosed in a protective casing, or cocoon. (pp. 9, 13, 16)